THE BAD GUYS

EPISODE 1   **EPISODE 2**

SCHOLASTIC

• FOR MY BOYS •

Scholastic Children's Books
An imprint of Scholastic Ltd
Euston House, 24 Eversholt Street, London, NW1 1DB, UK
Registered office: Westfield Road, Southam, Warwickshire, CV47 0RA
SCHOLASTIC and associated logos are trademarks and/or
registered trademarks of Scholastic Inc.

Bad Guys Episode 1 first published in Australia by Scholastic Australia, 2015
First published in the UK by Scholastic Ltd, 2015
Bad Guys Episode 2 first published in Australia by Scholastic Australia, 2015
First published in the UK by Scholastic Ltd, 2016
This edition first published 2018

Text copyright © Aaron Blabey, 2015

The right of Aaron Blabey to be identified as the author and illustrator of
this work has been asserted by him.

ISBN 978 1407 18681 8

A CIP catalogue record for this book
is available from the British Library.

Printed by CPI Group (UK) Ltd, Croydon, CR0 4YY
Papers used by Scholastic Children's Books are made
from wood grown in sustainable forests.

1 3 5 7 9 10 8 6 4 2

www.scholastic.co.uk

AARON BLABEY

THE BAD GUYS

EPISODE 1

GOOD DEEDS.

WHETHER YOU LIKE
IT OR NOT.

• CHAPTER 1 •
MR. WOLF

Pssst!
Hey, you!

Get over here.

I said **GET OVER HERE**.

What's the problem?

Oh, I see.

Yeah, I get it . . .

You're thinking, "Ooooooh, it's a big, bad, scary wolf! I don't want to talk to him!

He's a **MONSTER**."

Grandma?

Well, let me tell you something, buddy –
Just because I've got

BIG POINTY TEETH

and

RAZOR-SHARP CLAWS

... and I *occasionally* like to dress up
like an **OLD LADY**, that doesn't mean ...

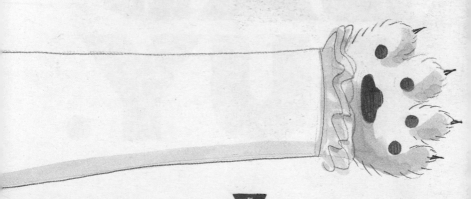

. . . I'm a

BAD
GUY.

METROPOLITAN
POLICE DEPARTMENT
SUSPECT RAP SHEET

Name: Mr. Wolf

Case Number: 102 451A

Alias: Big Bad, Mr. Choppers, Grandma

Address: The Woods

Known Associates: None

Criminal Activity:

* Blowing down houses (the three pigs involved were too scared to press charges)

* Impersonating sheep

* Breaking into the homes of old women

* Impersonating old women

* Attempting to eat old women

* Attempting to eat relatives of old women

* Theft of night gowns and slippers

Status: Dangerous. DO NOT APPROACH.

It's all **LIES**, I tell you.

But you don't believe me, do you?

Because I'm the Bad Guy, right?

I'm a great guy. A *nice* guy, even.

But I'm not just talking about **ME** . . .

I've got some buddies who have the same problem, so I've asked them to join us.

Any minute now, they'll be walking right through that door.

They're great guys. But just like me, they are **MISUNDERSTOOD**.

So don't go anywhere, OK?

· CHAPTER 2 ·
THE GANG

OK. Are you ready
to learn the truth?

You'd better be, baby.

Let's see who's here,
shall we?

Heeey! Look who it is!
It's my good pal,

MR. SNAKE.

You're going to *love* him.
He's a real . . .

. . . sweetheart.

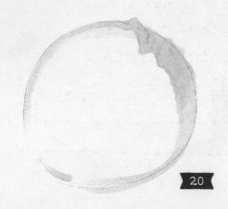

METROPOLITAN POLICE DEPARTMENT
SUSPECT RAP SHEET

Name: Mr. Snake

Case Number: 354 22C

Alias: The Chicken Swallower

Address: Unknown

Known Associates: None

Criminal Activity: * Broke into Mr. Ho's Pet Store

* Ate all the mice at Mr. Ho's Pet Store

* Ate all the canaries at Mr. Ho's Pet Store

* Ate all the guinea pigs at Mr. Ho's Pet Store

* Tried to eat Mr. Ho at Mr. Ho's Pet Store

* Tried to eat the doctor who tried to save Mr. Ho

* Tried to eat the policemen who tried to
save the doctor who tried to save Mr. Ho

* Ate the police dog who tried to save the
policemen who tried to save the doctor
who tried to save Mr. Ho

Status: Very dangerous. DO NOT APPROACH.

Look at this face!
Is this the face of a monster?

I don't think so.

This is **ONE SWEET GUY**.

Will this take long, man?
I've got mice to eat.

HA HA
HA HA!

What a joker this guy is!

"I've got mice to eat!"
That's a good one.

What a wise guy.

HA HA HA.

HA.

HA.

23

Take it easy.
Have a cupcake.

A cupcake?
You got
any mice?

Enough with the mice,
or I'll

EAT
YOU!

Goodness,
I wonder who could be
at the door?

27

Well, well. If it isn't

MR. PIRANHA.

Now, if anyone has
a bad reputation,
it's this guy . . .

Hola.

METROPOLITAN POLICE DEPARTMENT
SUSPECT RAP SHEET

Name: Mr. Piranha

Case Number: 775 906T

Alias: The Butt Biter

Address: Tropical Rivers

Known Associates: The Piranha Brothers Gang, 900,543 members, all related to Mr. Piranha

Criminal Activity:

* Eating tourists

Status: EXTREMELY dangerous. DO NOT APPROACH.

I'm

HUNGRY.

You got any seals?

METROPOLITAN POLICE DEPARTMENT

SUSPECT RAP SHEET

Name: Mr. Shark

Case Number: 666 885E

Alias: Jaws

Address: Popular Tourist Destinations

* Will literally eat ANYTHING or ANYBODY.

Status: RIDICULOUSLY DANGEROUS. RUN!
SWIM! DON'T EVEN READ THIS!
GET OUT OF HERE!!

See?! This is what I'm talking about!
How will anyone take us seriously as

GOOD GUYS

if all you want to do is

EAT EVERYONE?

What am I **TALKING** about?
Well, sit down and I'll explain.

And that means *you*, too.

· CHAPTER 3 ·
the GOOD GUYS CLUB

AAAAHHHHHHH!!!!!!

Typical . . .

I'll be
wherever
I want.

Got it?

Me too, *chico*.

See? This is why
I don't work with fish.

44

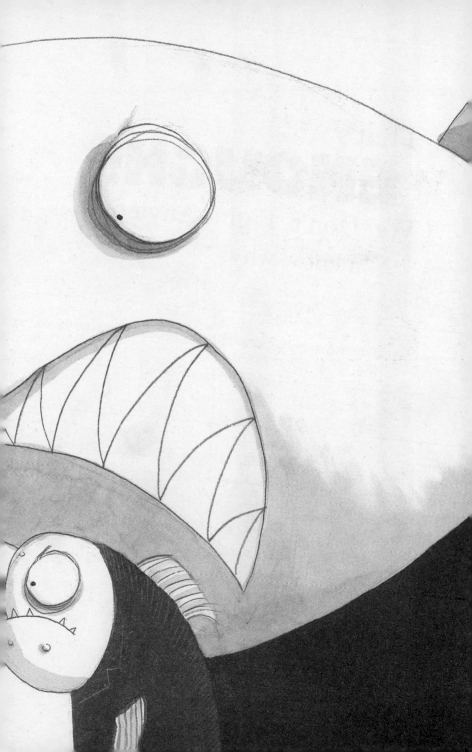

Because **THIS** is the very first meeting of . . .

THE
GOOD
GUYS
CLUB!

That's right!

The
GOOD
GUYS
CLUB!

I beg your pardon?

You heard me.

Aren't you tired of being the **VILLAIN?**

Aren't you tired of the **SCREAMS?**

Aren't you tired of the **FEAR?**

Not particularly.

Not in the slightest.

OF COURSE YOU ARE!

And I have the solution!

POP QUIZ!

Let's say we find a cat stuck in a tree.

What do we do?

You're kidding, right?

This guy's *loco*.

No, I'm not!

I'm a GENIUS!

And I'm going to make us all

HEROES!

You'll be glad you did, Mr. Piranha.

And so will you, Mr. Shark.

This is going to be **AWESOME**.

Now, everybody climb aboard!

And let's go do some

GOOD!

CHAPTER 4
CRUISING FOR TROUBLE

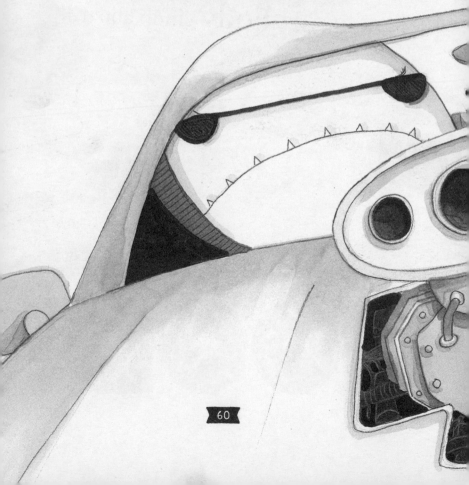

Hey, man, why are we driving around in this stupid car?
STUPID CAR?!

This car is a fuel-injected,

200-HORSEPOWER,

rock 'n' rollin' chariot of
flaming **COOLNESS**, my friend.
If we're going to be good guys,
don't you think we should
LOOK GOOD, too?

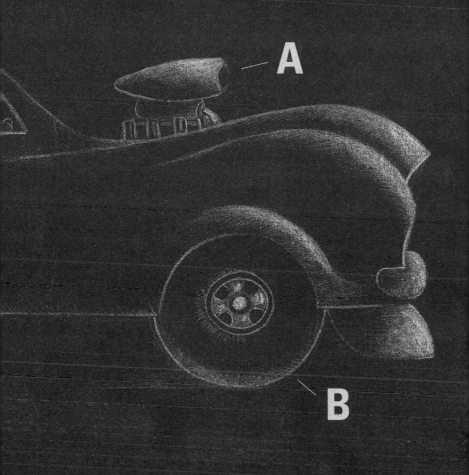

A - Wicked powerful V8 engine that runs on undiluted panther pee.

B - Fat wheels for just looking insanely cool.

C - Custom ejector seats for personal safety and also practical jokes.

D - Oversized muffler for being very, very loud at all times.

And it's roomy, too!

Hey, it's a sweet ride, *chico*. But I get carsick, man. So, what ARE we doing out here?

HEY!

What's the big deal, *chico*?
Car travel makes me
let off a little gas.

SO WHAT?

GOOD BOY

Actually,
that feels
real nice.

Seriously though, man . . .
what are we looking for?

SCREEECH!

THAT
is what we're looking for,
Mr. Snake!

· CHAPTER 5 ·
HERE, KITTY

So, what are we going to do?

Rescue the cat.

And what are we **NOT** going to do?

Eat the cat.

THAT'S RIGHT! I don't know about you, but I feel PUMPED!

OK, now let's do this thing . . .

What was *that*? Are you trying to give him a heart attack?

WHAT? I was, like, being totally cool . . .

Let me handle this.

HEY, YOU!
Get down here,
or I'll **SHIMMY** up that tree and **BITE** you on your **FURRY LITTLE BUTT!**

This is not what
I had in mind.

SWING!!

HEY!

Where's the piranha?

I don't know
what you're
talking about.

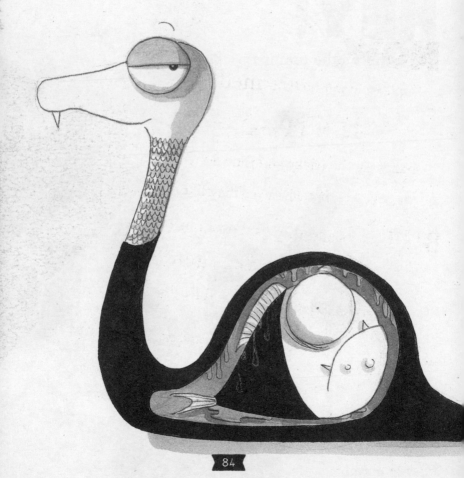

NOW,

please don't be alarmed.

It's true,

snakes can be tricky and they do tend to

swallow whatever they like.

BUT — luckily, they swallow things *whole*

and I happen to know a gentle,

harmless technique that'll fix this right up.

Excuse me for one moment . . .

I SAID . . .

WHERE'S

THE PIRANHA?!

...EOW!

THAT'S IT!
I've got you,
I've got you . . .

· CHAPTER 6 ·
THE PLAN

Nice work.
High fives,
all around!

You're the only
one with hands.

Our first mission.

It's time for

OPERATION DOG POUND!

THE

534 10

200 DOGS

DOG POUND

20 GUARDS

ONE WAY IN.
ONE WAY OUT.

IRON BARS!
RAZOR WIRE!
BAD FOOD!

96

There are **200** puppies locked up in the

MAXIMUM SECURITY CITY DOG POUND.

Their hopes and dreams are trapped
behind walls of stone and bars of steel.

But guess what?

We're going to

SET THEM FREE!

We couldn't get a kitten out of a tree. How are we supposed to bust out 200 dogs?

It's easy! One of us just has to get in there and open the cages!

And how do we do that?

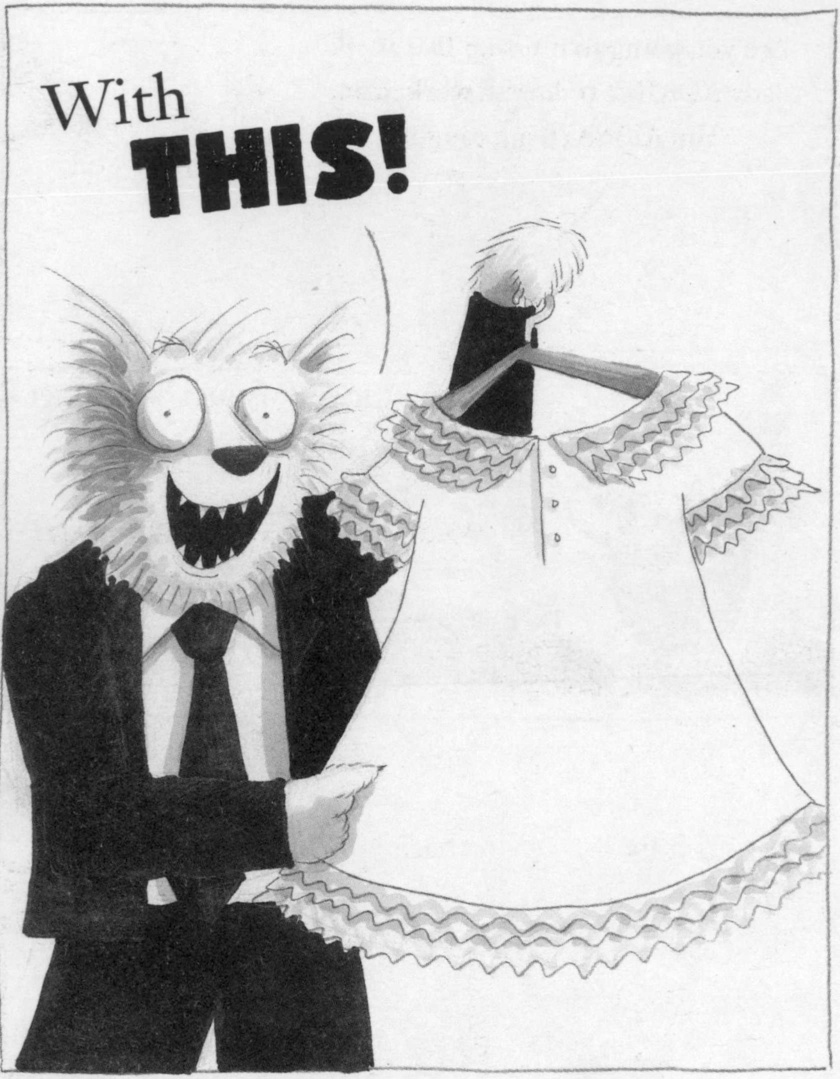
With
THIS!

Are you going to dress up like an old lady AGAIN? It doesn't work, man. You ALWAYS get caught!

Who said anything about *me*?

CHAPTER 7

THE POUND

Hello?
Oh, certainly, miss.
I'll buzz you in.

BUZZZ!

Now, what can I do
for . . . uh . . . you?

I'm just a pretty young lady who has lost her dog.
Please, oh please, can you help me, sir?

He's in!
I **KNEW** this
would work.

Now, you know what to do.
Once those cages are open,
we won't have long,
so don't mess it up.

Climb aboard, fellas!

What's that
thing for?

Never mind. Just hold on tight.
And remember — once Mr. Shark
gives me the signal, I'll get you
inside and all you have to do is tell
the dogs which way to run.

GOT IT?

Yeah. But
how do we
get inside?

But don't worry!

I have **EXCELLENT** aim

and I'm **85%** sure

that I'll get you in on my first throw —

THAT'S

how confident I am!

You know, I wouldn't normally open all these cages at once, but since you asked so nicely . . .

BOO HOO!
BOO HOO!
BOO HOO!
That's the signal!
Hey, man, can we talk about this for a second?

There's no time to talk! Hold on tight, little buddies.

It's time . . .

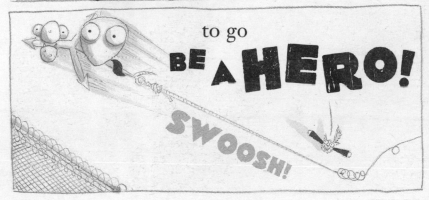

OK.
Best out of three.

YEAH.
I'm getting the
hang of it now . . .

SPLAT!

If we survive this, I'm going to *eat* that wolf.

WHOOOSH!

Not if I do first.

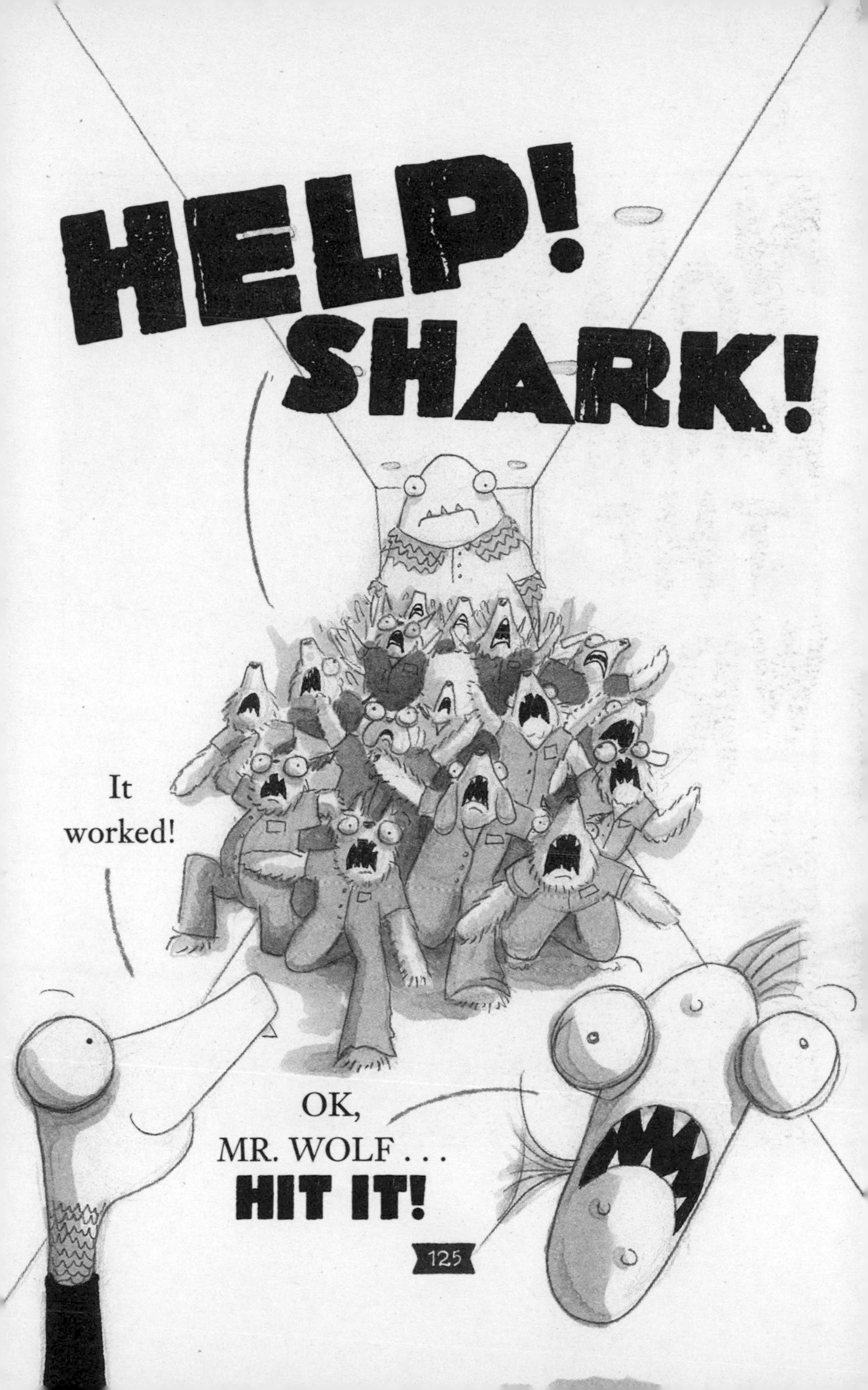
HELP! SHARK!
It worked!
OK,
MR. WOLF . . .
HIT IT!

I hear you,
little buddy.

Let's give those puppies their . . .

127

And a SHARK!
And a SNAKE!
And possibly some kind of VAMPIRE SARDINE!
224

· CHAPTER 8 ·
SO, HOW ABOUT IT?

I'm not a SARDINE! I'M A PIRANHA, man! **PIRANHA!**

Whatever.

You're missing the point, guys. **WE DID IT!** We gave 200 dogs a whole new life. Doesn't that make you feel **AWESOME?!**

You really do hug WAY more than I'm comfortable with, man.

Aw, **C'MON!**

You loved it! I KNOW you did!

Tell me the truth — didn't it feel great

to be the **GOOD GUY** for once?

Tell me how it felt, fellas . . .

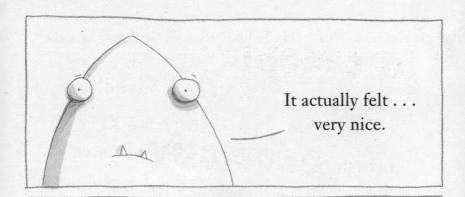

It actually felt . . .
very nice.

It felt better than nice.
It felt . . . good.

It felt **WONDERFUL**,
man. But they still called me
a SARDINE!!!

If you stick with me, little buddy, no one will ever mistake you for a sardine ever again! You'll be Bolivia's most famous hero! Are you with me?

Sure. But you'd better be right, *chico*.

And what about you, big fella?

I . . . I really liked being good. I'm in.

That just leaves you, handsome. What do you say? Want to be in my gang?

Only if I have your word that there'll be no more hugging.

I'll try, baby! But I'm not making any promises!

Today is the first day of our new lives.

We are not Bad Guys anymore.

WE'RE GOOD GUYS!

And we are going to make the world a better place.

TO BE CONTINUED . . .

GUESS WHAT?

The **BAD GUYS** haven't even warmed up.

Freeing 200 dogs is **NOTHING**.

How about rescuing **10,000 chickens** from a **high-tech cage farm** protected by the world's most **unbeatable** laser security system?

BUT how do you rescue chickens when one of you is known as **The Chicken Swallower?**

Join the **BAD GUYS** when they return for more shady **good deeds** with a new, creepy member of the team . . . and keep your eyes peeled for the **SUPER VILLAIN** who just might be the end of them.

The **BAD GUYS** in
Mission Unpluckable
COMING SOON!

AARON BLABEY

THE BAD GUYS

EPISODE 2 MISSION UNPLUCKABLE

NEWS FLASH!

PANIC AT THE DOG POUND!

We interrupt this program to bring you a breaking news story.

TIFFANY FLUFFIT is our reporter on the scene. Tiffany, what can you tell us?

CHUCK MELON

Thanks, Chuck!

Well, there have been **SHOCKING** scenes at the **DOG POUND** today.

It seems some kind of **CRAZED GANG** burst in, smashed down a wall, and then drove away in a very loud hot-rod car, causing **200 TERRIFIED PUPPY DOGS** to run away in fright.

TIFFANY FLUFFIT 6 NEWS

I have with me **MR. GRAHAM PLONKER**,
Chief of Dog Pound Security.

Mr. Plonker, how would you describe these
MONSTERS?

Uh . . . well . . . it all happened so
fast, but . . . I'm pretty sure there
were four of them . . .

I mean, there was definitely a **WOLF**.

EXCLUSIVE FOOTAGE!

A really *mean*-looking wolf, with pointy teeth.

And there was a **SNAKE**.

HAVE YOU SEEN THIS SNAKE?

A very *ugly* snake, who also seemed very cranky for some reason . . .

Uh, then there was a **YOUNG LADY** . . .

PRETTY GIRL? OR DEADLY SHARK?

. . . or possibly a gigantic **SHARK**. It was hard to tell which . . .

Oh yeah, and there was also some kind of nasty little fish.

MUTANT SARDINE ON THE LOOSE!

Maybe a **SARDINE**.

Not sure.

But, Mr. Plonker, would
you say that these
villains seemed . . .

DANGEROUS?

Oh yes, Tiffany. They're
dangerous, all right.

In fact, I'd say we are dealing
with some *serious* . . .

LIVE FROM THE DOG POUND 6 NEWS

· CHAPTER 1 ·
OK, LET'S TRY THAT AGAIN

What's that guy talking about?
We **SAVED** those puppy dogs!
It was a

RESCUE!

We're the **GOOD GUYS** here!

AND FOR THE LAST TIME,
I AM **NOT** A SARDINE!

I'M A
PIRANHA!

MUNCH! MUNCH!

MUNCH!

See, Wolf? No one is **EVER** going to believe we're good guys. I'm getting out of here before the cops come looking for us.

Oh, **NO** you don't, Mr. Snake! We're not going to quit now. We're just getting started.

Don't forget **HOW GOOD** it felt to
rescue those dogs!

All we need to do now is make sure that
everyone can **SEE** that we're **HEROES**.

We just need to do something
SO AWESOME that the whole
world will sit up and take notice!

What did you have in
mind, Mr. Wolf?

Well, take a look INSIDE
Sunnyside Chicken Farm, fellas.

10,000 CHICKENS!

Stuffed into **TINY** cages!

24 hours a day!

With **NO** sunlight!

And **NO** room to run and play!

But that's awful!
That's the worst thing
I've ever heard!

What are we waiting for?!

**WE NEED TO SET THOSE
LITTLE CHICKIE-BABIES
FREE!**

Let's go! Let's go! Let's go!
Let's go! Let's go! Let's go!
Let's go! Let's go! Let's go!
Let's go! Let's go! Let's go!
LET'S GO!

Well, *hellooooo* . . .

Are you OK, man?

Huh?

DROOL

Oh yeah . . . sorry.
I was just thinking that chickens are delicious—I mean, *DELIGHTFUL*—and I think we need to save them all **RIGHT NOW**.

Oh, if only it were that simple, my friend. But I'm afraid I have some bad news . . .

Sunnyside Chicken Farm is

IMPOSSIBLE

to break into!

It's a **MAXIMUM SECURITY CHICKEN FARM** with **STEEL WALLS** that are 30 feet high and 8 feet thick!

There are **NO WINDOWS** and all the doors are **HEAVILY GUARDED.**

SUNNYSIDE INC.

And even if you *did* get inside, you'd be caught instantly because . . .

If you touch the FLOOR, an **ALARM** goes off!

If you touch the WALLS, an **ALARM** goes off!

And if you walk into the LASER BEAMS, an **ALARM** goes off!

• FLOOR ALARMS

• WALL ALARMS

• LASER ALARMS

Did you say
LASER BEAMS?
Why are you even showing us this, *chico*? We don't have the skills to pull off a job like this!

No, we don't.
But I know a guy who does.

Who?

· CHAPTER 2 ·
the FREAKY GEEK

Hey, dudes! It's totally
awesome to meet you!

**Aieeeeee!
RUN** *CHICOS*! It's a
TARANTULA!!!

I'm sorry about this, Legs.
I don't know what's
wrong with them.

Aw, it's cool.
Happens all the time.

LEGS?!

You *know* this monster?!

What were you thinking,
bringing a tarantula into
our clubhouse?

. . . *Can't breathe* . . .
spider . . .
Mommy . . .
Mommy . . .
I want my mommy . . .

Mr. Shark! Pull yourself together!
You guys should be ASHAMED of yourselves!
LEGS is just like us.
He's a GOOD GUY with a BAD reputation.

Aw, thanks,
Wolfie.

He's **DANGEROUS,** man.

Yeah!
And why isn't he
wearing any pants?

I don't do pants, dude. I like to feel free.

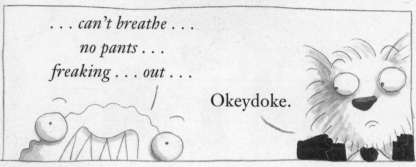

. . . can't breathe . . .
no pants . . .
freaking . . . out . . .

Okeydoke.

Legs? Why don't you
show them what you can do?

OK. Let's start with something simple.

TAP! TAP! TAP! TAP! TAP! TAP! TAP!

ACCESS: GRANTED
Name: MR. SNAKE
Status: Very Dangerous
Action: Do Not Approach

Hey! That's my police file!

Geez, they don't like you very much, do they?

But **NOBODY** can access that! There's no way you can hack into their system. That's the toughest security there is!

Yeah, it *is* kind of tricky.

But it's worth it just to see you smile, Mr. Snake.

Not for a **SUPERHACKER** like Legs!
He's a computer **GENIUS**. And he has a
plan that will get us inside that chicken farm.

Thanks, Wolfie. But first,
I'd better put this back
the way I found it. We are
good guys, after all . . .

. . . and I wouldn't like
to get us in trouble.
Sorry, Mr. Snake.
You're *dangerous* again,
I'm afraid.

Hey!

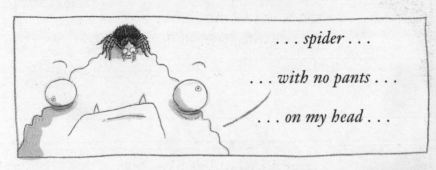

This is **SO** cool, guys! I'm so happy to be part of the team. And I bet by this time tomorrow, we're totally going to be **BESTIES!**
. . . *spider* . . .
. . . *with no pants* . . .
. . . *on my head* . . .
FAINT!
Hey, *chico*. I got one word for you—*pants*.
SPLAT!

• CHAPTER 3 •
MISSION, LIKE, TOTALLY IMPOSSIBLE

OK, dudes, I took your advice and found myself some clothes. What do you think?

I can still see his

BIG FURRY BUTT.

Cut it out,
Piranha.
Just listen
to him.

OK.

To get you guys inside
Sunnyside Chicken Farm,
all I need to do is hack into
their main computer and
switch off all the alarms.

BUT

there's a problem . . .

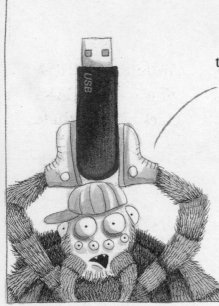

The security is **SO HIGH** that I can't do it from here.

I need you guys to plug **THIS THING** into their computer, so I can access it.

Once you do that, I can SHUT IT ALL DOWN and get you to those chickens.

Wait a minute. You're telling us that you can hack into my police file, but you **CAN'T** get into a CHICKEN FARM without our help?

Yeah. It's WEIRD.
This is one SCARY
chicken farm, dude.

But if it's so scary, how do we
get to the computer?
Wolf said there's no way into
the building!

Well, there is **ONE** way.

But it sure isn't easy . . .

There's a **SMALL HATCH** on the roof.

You'll need to go through the hatch and **DROP** 150 feet on a rope to the computer below. Once you get to it, **JUST PLUG ME IN**.

BUT!

If you touch the WALLS or the FLOOR, the **ALARMS** will go off and you'll get caught.

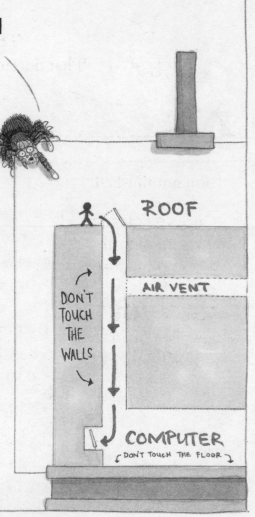

ROOF

AIR VENT

DON'T TOUCH THE WALLS

COMPUTER

DON'T TOUCH THE FLOOR

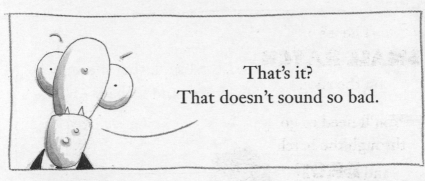

That's it?
That doesn't sound so bad.

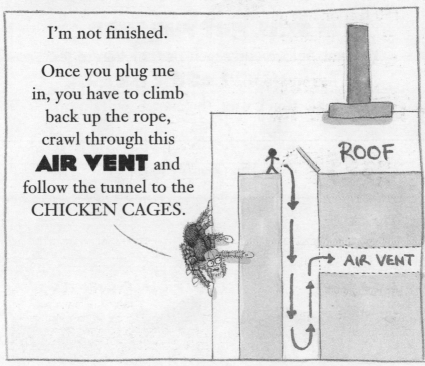

I'm not finished.

Once you plug me in, you have to climb back up the rope, crawl through this **AIR VENT** and follow the tunnel to the CHICKEN CAGES.

ROOF

AIR VENT

Like I said, that doesn't
sound so bad.

I'M STILL NOT FINISHED.
You see, before you reach the chicken cages,
you'll come to the **LASER BEAMS**.
And if you touch one, the alarms will go off.

Oh, and they'll zap you.
And they *really* hurt.

LASERS

→ AIR VENT →

 But why are the lasers still on?
I thought you were going to shut
down all the alarms.

 I will.
The **OTHER** alarms will be off.

But the **LASER ALARMS**
can only be turned off by hand.
You have to flick a switch
once you're inside.

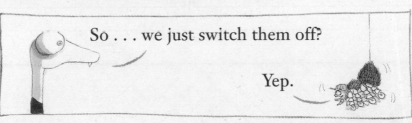 So . . . we just switch them off?

Yep.

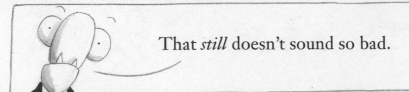 That *still* doesn't sound so bad.

That's because I'm **STILL NOT FINISHED!**

The switch is on the OTHER SIDE of the laser beams, so you have to GO **THROUGH** THEM to reach it!

CHICKENS THIS WAY

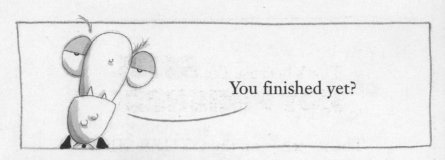

You finished yet?

Uhhh . . . yep.

Good! Because that sounds **LOCO!** There's **NO WAY** we can pull this off, man!

Oh yes, we can!

But **ONLY** if we work as a **TEAM!**

So, Snake and Piranha—
you guys are coming with ME!

We are going to **GET INSIDE**,

plug **THIS THING** into the computer, and

GET TO THOSE CHICKENS!

This is going to be

GREAT!

But . . . what about me?

You're going to be working with me, Big Guy.
It's OUR JOB to get these guys in and out of there safely!
Isn't this awesome? You and I are going to SPEND A
LOT OF TIME TOGETHER!

*Oh . . . that's . . .
great . . . but . . .
I think . . .
I'm going . . .
to cry . . .*

189

No time for tears, Mr. Shark.

WE'VE GOT CHICKENS TO SAVE!

· CHAPTER 4 ·
DOWN THE HATCH

Hey, what are you guys doing
all the way over there?

LATER THAT NIGHT...

SUNNYSIDE
CHICKEN FARM
KEEP OUT!

SUNNYSIDE
INC.

We look ridiculous.

Hey, Tarantula! What's with the stupid suits?

Shhh! Not so loud, Mr. Piranha. These suits are GREAT! They'll keep you cool and make you really hard to spot.

PLUS!

Each suit has a microphone and earpiece, so we can all talk to each other.

GOT IT?

Hey, Wolf, do you really promise there'll be chickens down there?

It's a **CHICKEN** FARM! Of course there'll be chickens. Why are you so worried about that?

Oh, no reason.

I just really **LOVE** chickens, man.

They're so nice to eat— I mean, they're so nice to *MEET*.

Yeah . . .

 You DO understand that we're here to SAVE the chickens, don't you?

 Uh-huh.

 And you wouldn't try to **EAT** any chickens, would you?

 Uh-uh.

 Hey! Can we just DO THIS? My jumpsuit is chafing.

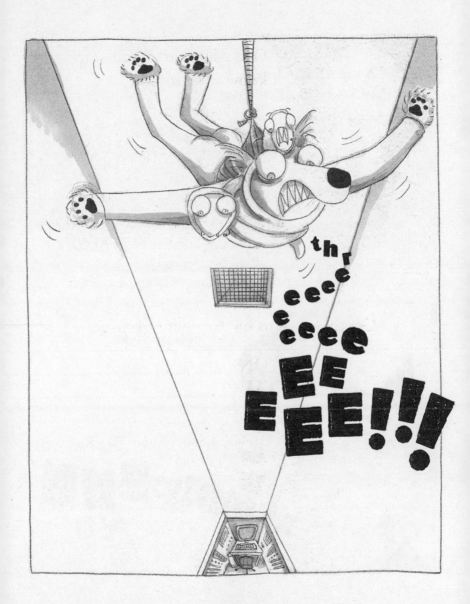

OK. OK. OK. Well, the walls are a *little* closer than I expected.

Mr. Shark! Whatever you do, make sure you lower us *SLOWLY*.

I hear you.

BOING!

Do you need a hand, Big Buddy?

EEEEEEEEE

FOOF!

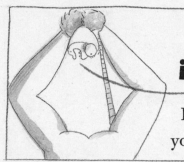

Whoa. That was close.

¡AY, CARAMBA!
Mr. Wolf?
Has anyone ever told you that
your face looks like a **BUTT?**

Oh. Sorry. My mistake.

What?

Hey, look! The computer!
I think I can reach it . . .

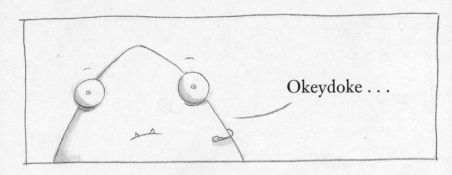

Okeydoke . . .

NO! WAIT!

Look what he's eating, *chicos*.
That's a sardine sandwich.

I think I have an idea.

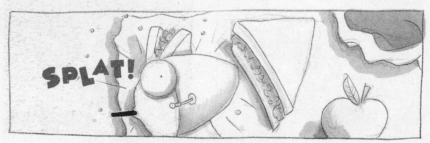

WIGGLE!

WIGGLE!
WIGGLE!

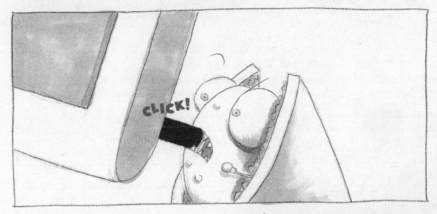

CLICK!

I don't believe it! HE DID IT!

He sure did, dudes. I'm in!

And . . .

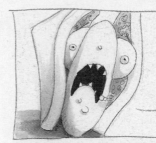

This was a one-way ticket, *chico*.

WHAT? We can't just leave you behind!

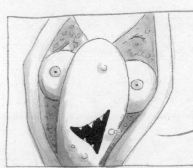

You have to, *hermanos*.
There is no other way.

Go and save those little
chickens, man.
Save them for **ME!**

Wolf! Snap out of it!
SHARK! Pull us up!

You got it.

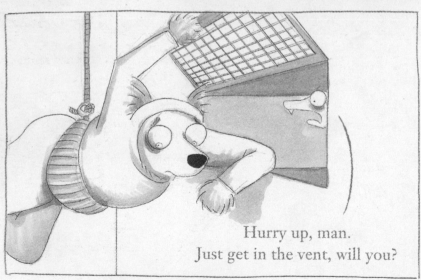

Hurry up, man.
Just get in the vent, will you?

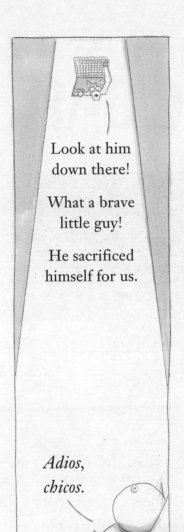

Look at him down there!

What a brave little guy!

He sacrificed himself for us.

Adios, chicos.

Yeah, yeah. Let's do this. I'm starving—I mean, I'm *STARTING* to want to save some chickens. Yep.

You're right. We should go.

Adios, Mr. Piranha.

Stay safe.

Easy for you to say, baby.

· CHAPTER 5 ·
MIND THE GAP

See, Mr. Snake?
This is what I've been talking about—
without Mr. Piranha, we would **NEVER**
have made it this far. **THAT'S** what
being on a team is all about.

COOPERATION.

Yeah, yeah, yeah, that's *so*
interesting, but WHERE ARE
THE CHICKENS, man?

Just up ahead, I'd say.

This bit has been a lot easier
than I thought. I really don't
know what all the fuss was ab—

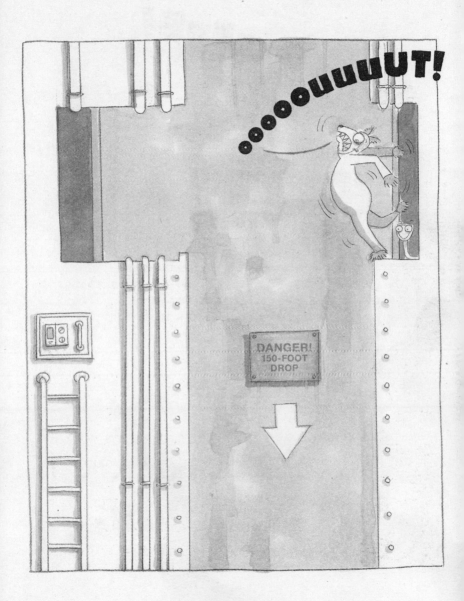

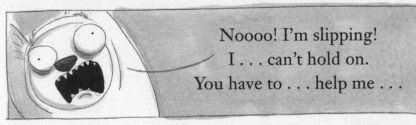

You need to go
on a diet, man.
You really do.

Now, let's think.

What do we do?

We're trapped.

It's not just ME
that's trapped. And
it's not just YOU.
It's **US**.

We're trapped as
a **TEAM**. So we
need to get out of
this as a **TEAM**.

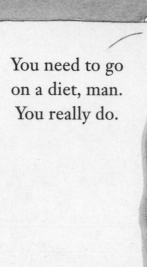

I'VE **GOT** IT!

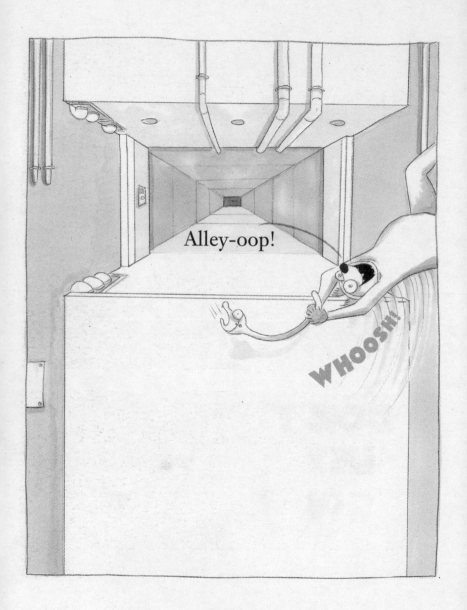

• CHAPTER 6 •
LET'S START OVER

That's not good.

Piranha?
Can you hear me?

Mr. Shark? Is that you?

I'm about to be a monkey's lunch here, man.

You sit tight, Mr. P. I'm coming to get you.

BOING!

Can I help, BIG FELLA?

Really . . . scared . . . of . . . spiders . . .

Uh-huh. And why is that?
It's OK, you can tell me.

OK, well . . .
you're **FREAKY** to look at because
you have **TOO MANY EYES** and
TOO MANY LEGS
and I'm SO creeped
out by you that
**I MIGHT
THROW UP!**

But . . . I'm sorry if that
sounds rude.

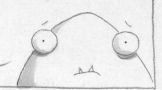

It's OK.

No, really. I feel terrible saying
that. You must think I'm awful.

No, that's OK.
You seem like a nice guy.
But can I ask you one little thing?

Yes, of course.

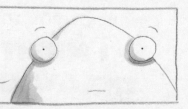

Well . . .

since I can't help being a tarantula in the same way that you CAN'T HELP BEING A

MASSIVE, TERRIFYING SEA MONSTER,

I wonder if you could just

GET OVER IT

and then

MAYBE

I could help you rescue your friend!

Um . . . OK.

I'm so sorry. That was really uncool.

It's OK. That's good advice.

Well . . . um . . . how are we going to rescue that piranha?

I've heard you're pretty good at disguises. Is that right?

I have my moments.

OK, well, I'm REALLY good at making stuff. So why don't we work together?

OK.

But what kind of disguise is going to get me inside a chicken farm?

Why don't you pull the feathers out of those pillows there, Mr. Shark, and I'll tell you my idea.

· CHAPTER 7 ·
TRUST ME, I'M A SNAKE

Oh no! Look at those laser beams! I'll **NEVER** get through!

I think we have a problem.

CAGE ➡

231

Ooooh no, no, no, no. There's no problem—I'll fit through those lasers. I'll just have to handle this one **ALONE.**

Are you sure?

Oh, ABSOLUTELY.
I'll just wriggle my way across and have a chicken feast—I mean . . . I'll get those chickens **RELEASED.**

Yeah.
Released.
Heh heh.

But you'll switch off the lasers when you get across?

Yeah, yeah, sure.

You take your time, little buddy!

YOU ROCK!

I'm just SO proud of these guys.

WHISTLE
WHISTLE

Geez, it's been fifteen minutes.

Are you OK over there, Mr. Snake?

Aha! He's done it.

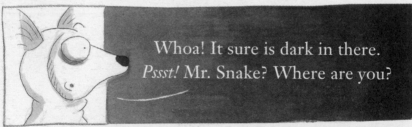

Whoa! It sure is dark in there. *Pssst!* Mr. Snake? Where are you?

Oh, there you are! Is everything OK?

Urghugh.

Mr. Snake?

What are you doing
over there?

In the dark?

Behind all those . . .
EMPTY cages?

Gnnughgagh.

You sound funny, man.
Are you OK?

Sgllurrr!

Oh no.

Wait a minute—
You didn't—

SNAKE?!
WHAT DID
YOU DO?!!

Oh, I don't think so.

Snake, you are *not* going to ruin this plan. No, you are not.

Huh?

GRAB!

NO. YOU. ARE. NOT.

• CHAPTER 8 •
WHOLE LOTTA CHICKEN

Who knows? But let's get it back down to the cages.

Oh, sorry! I interrupted your lunch . . .

Aw, that's OK. I can eat on the run.

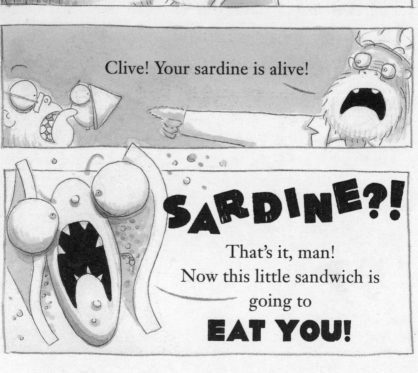

ARRGGHHH!!!

Yeah, I'm your **WORST** nightmare, *hombre*! I'm a piranha burger with **EXTRA SPICE!**

Mr. Shark? Is that you?

Yep.

Wow! I barely recognized you.

Yeah, I know.
I'm good at disguises.

WHOOP! WHOOP! WHOOP!

OH NO! They've set off the alarm!

WHOOP! WHOO

The alarm!
We have to hurry!

254

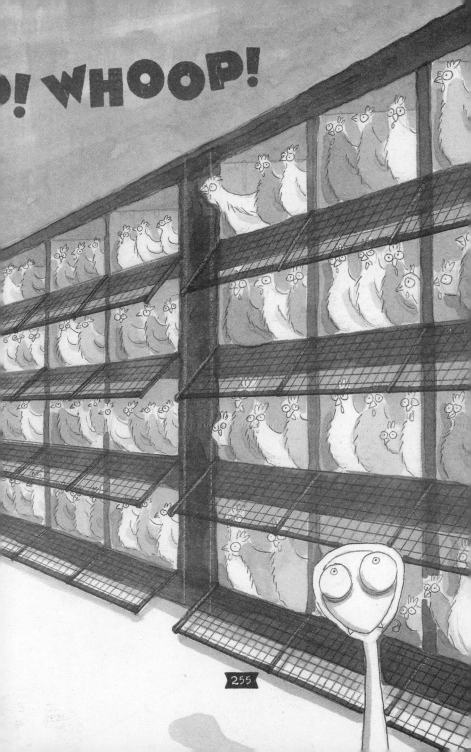

! WHOOP!

We've opened the cages,
but they won't run.
What's wrong with these
stupid chickens?

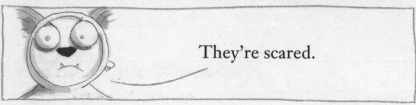

They're scared.

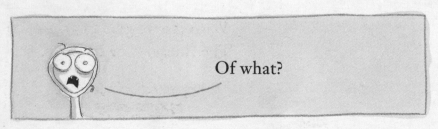

Of what?

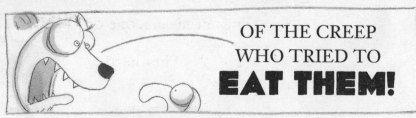

OF THE CREEP
WHO TRIED TO
EAT THEM!

I couldn't help it.

I'm sorry.

Yeah, well, "sorry" won't help us now, Mr. Snake.

What are we going to do? The chickens are terrified.

They need someone to **FOLLOW**.

They need someone to **TRUST**.

They need . . .

Wow. That's one big chicken.

All right, girls. I know you're scared, but this is your **ONE CHANCE** to get out of this horrible place.

Do you understand?

GOOD.

Run, little
chickies! Run!

THEN LET'S GET OUT OF HERE!

 Mr. Piranha!
You're here!

Are you OK?

 I'm completely coated
in mayonnaise.

 Oh. I see.

 It's not too bad, actually.

I kind of like it.

Throw me at him!
It's your only chance!

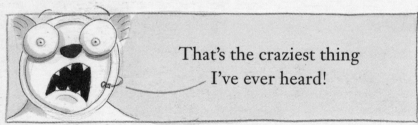

That's the craziest thing
I've ever heard!

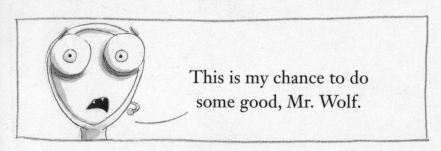

This is my chance to do
some good, Mr. Wolf.

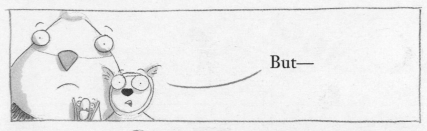

But—

THROW ME NOW OR THESE CHICKENS WILL NEVER BE FREE! **DO IT!**

And don't miss. **GOT IT?**

Got it.

Hi. Let's play a game. The first person to open the door doesn't get bitten by a snake.

You win.

Now, can I ask you to please lock all the guards in behind us after we leave?

Oh, and if you don't, I **WILL** find out where you live and you **WILL** find me in your bed in the middle of the night.

Do we have a deal?

Yes, we do.

Marvelous!

BOING!

See? You're not the only Good Guy around here . . .

I knew it! I knew it! I knew it!

OK. Less hugs. More escaping.

· CHAPTER 9 ·
WHAT A TEAM

I am so proud of you guys! **10,000** chickens are free because of **YOU!**

I think we're starting to get the hang of this hero thing, fellas.

And that means you, too, Mr. Snake.

OK, Huggy Bear. Let's not make a great big hairy deal out of it.

Aw, sure thing, you old grouch! Let's get out of here . . .

But . . .

What happened to the **CAR?!**

Oh yeah. While I was waiting for you guys to get back, I fitted it with **MONSTER TRUCK** tires and a **JET ENGINE**. I hope you don't mind?

We don't mind!

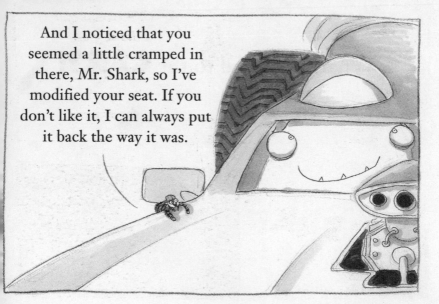

And I noticed that you seemed a little cramped in there, Mr. Shark, so I've modified your seat. If you don't like it, I can always put it back the way it was.

I . . . I *love* it, Legs. You're very thoughtful.

Thank you.

Anytime, Mr. Shark. Anytime at all.

I'm breathing.
It's all good.
I'm breathing.
It's all good.
I'm breathing.
It's all good.

SQUEAK!

Hey! Did anybody else hear that?

Hmmm.
It seems to be coming from that

CREEPY OLD HOUSE

next to the chicken farm that we . . .
somehow didn't notice. Perhaps it's
a chicken that's lost its way?

I didn't know chickens
could squeak . . .

Nope. My mistake.
There's nothing here. It's empty.

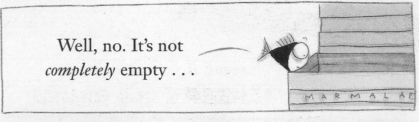

Well, no. It's not
completely empty . . .

Look!

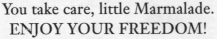

GOOD GUYS?

And just because they call themselves
GOOD GUYS, they think they can

BREAK INTO MY CHICKEN FARM AND SET MY CHICKENS FREE?!

AND THEY THINK THEY CAN
GET AWAY WITH IT?

Well, we'll see about that. I shall make them pay.

Oh yes . . .

I SHALL MAKE THEM PAY! HE HE HE HE HE HE! HE HE HE HE HE!

The **BAD GUYS** are doing some **GOOD** . . . whether you **WANT THEM TO OR NOT.**

Don't miss their first **heroic** adventure—breaking every last dog out of the pound!